MARTIN
AND THE
GIANT
LIONS

by CARON LEE COHEN

illustrated by ELIZABETH SAYLES

CLARION BOOKS • NEW YORK

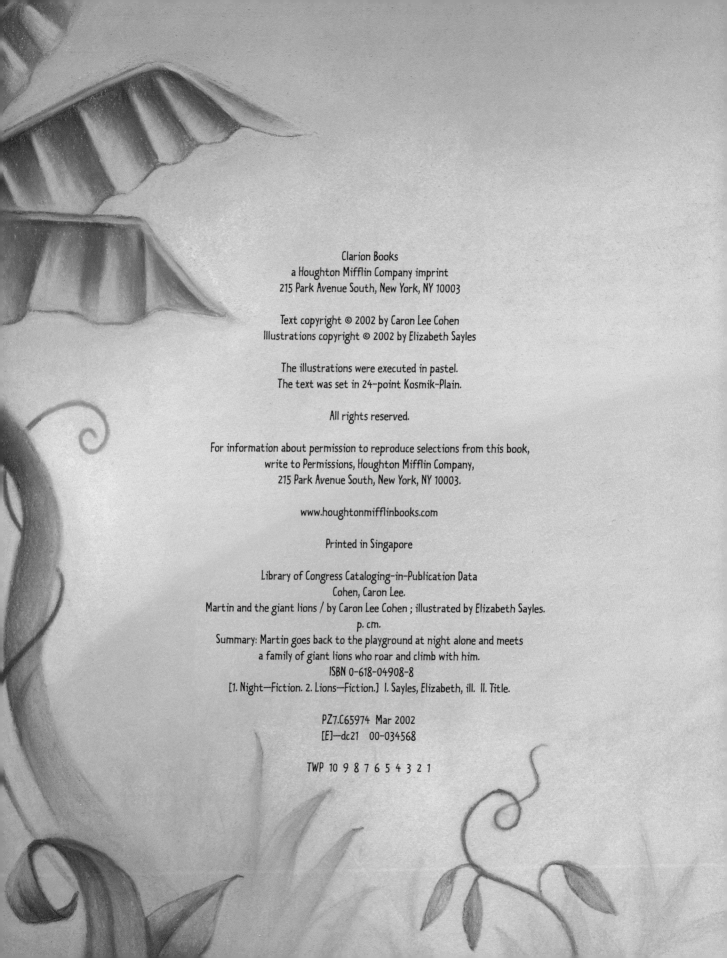

Clarion Books
a Houghton Mifflin Company imprint
215 Park Avenue South, New York, NY 10003

Text copyright © 2002 by Caron Lee Cohen
Illustrations copyright © 2002 by Elizabeth Sayles

The illustrations were executed in pastel.
The text was set in 24-point Kosmik-Plain.

www.houghtonmifflinbooks.com

Printed in Singapore

Library of Congress Cataloging-in-Publication Data
Cohen, Caron Lee.
Martin and the giant lions / by Caron Lee Cohen ; illustrated by Elizabeth Sayles.
p. cm.
Summary: Martin goes back to the playground at night alone and meets
a family of giant lions who roar and climb with him.
ISBN 0-618-04908-8
[1. Night—Fiction. 2. Lions—Fiction.] I. Sayles, Elizabeth, ill. II. Title.

PZ7.C65974 Mar 2002
[E]—dc21   00-034568

TWP 10 9 8 7 6 5 4 3 2 1

For Cecilia Irene Perlstein
and
Barbara Ford

—C.L.C.

For my father, whose wisdom
is never-ending

—E.S.

4

Rrrroooooaaaarrrr!

Martin always roared
when he climbed the giant jungle ladder.

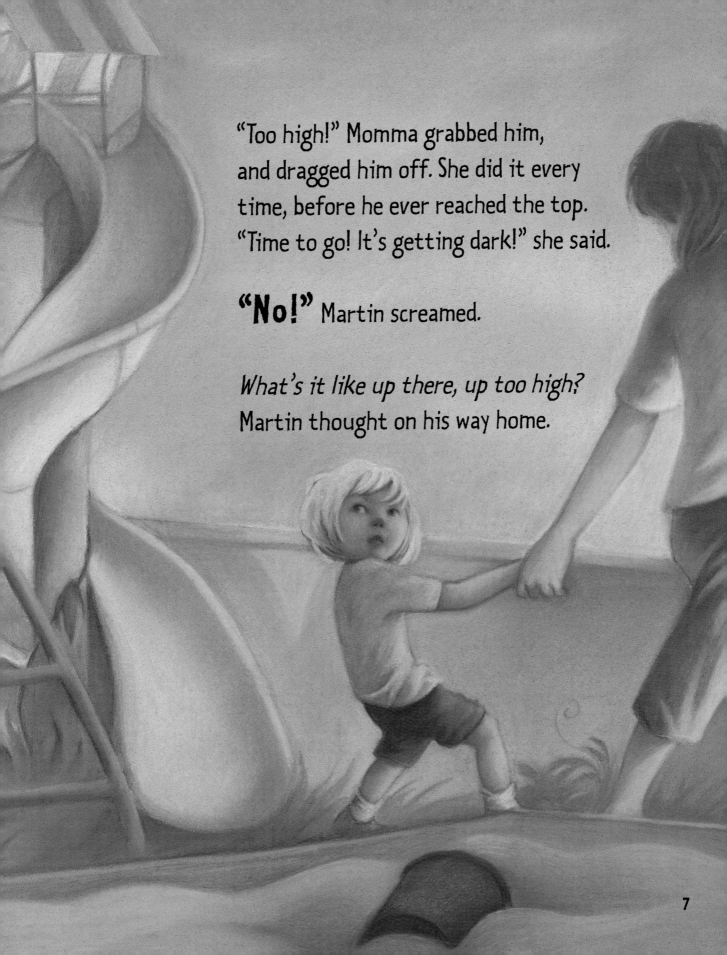

"Too high!" Momma grabbed him,
and dragged him off. She did it every
time, before he ever reached the top.
"Time to go! It's getting dark!" she said.

"No!" Martin screamed.

What's it like up there, up too high?
Martin thought on his way home.

What happens there in the dark after you kiss good night and go to sleep? That's what he was thinking when Momma hugged him and kissed him and said good night.

Then Martin looked out his window into the far dark night. More than anything he wanted to climb the giant jungle ladder way up high, all by himself, while the whole world slept.

"I'll bring back the night in my bucket,"
he said, and hopped on his purple truck,

vrooom, vrooom, vrooom,
vrooom,

vrooom

sailing away down the dark street,
around the sleeping town,
through the park hedge,
under the seesaw,
stopping at the sandbox.

Martin heard *growling.*
Then he saw—prowling—a giant lion family.

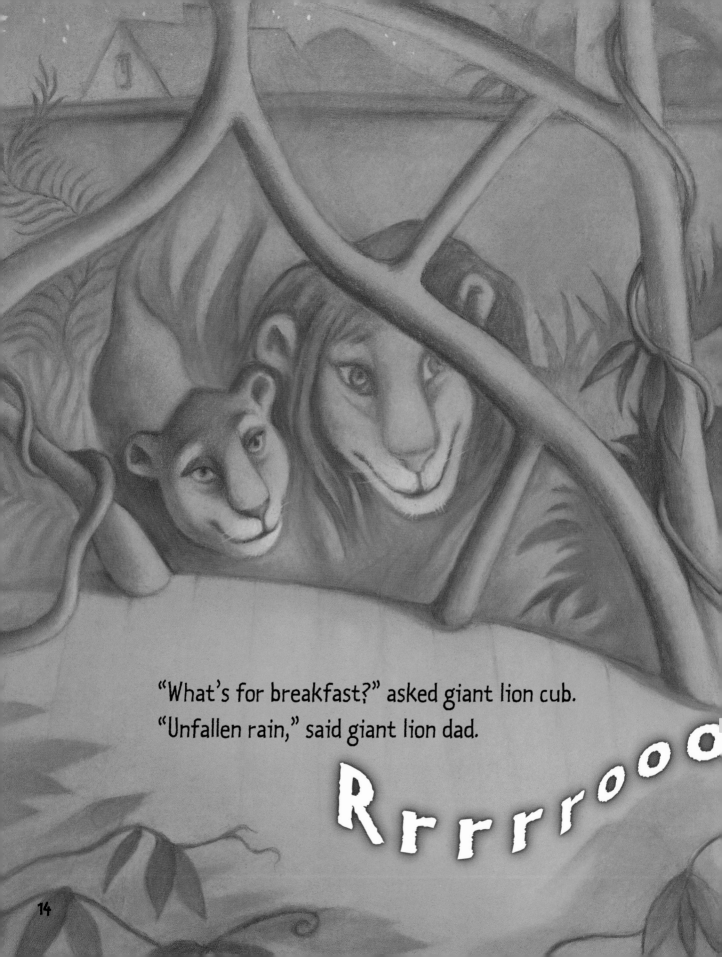

"What's for breakfast?" asked giant lion cub.
"Unfallen rain," said giant lion dad.

Rrrrrooo

So giant lion cub leaped up.
"Watch me. Watch me.
I'll get it way up high."

ooaaaaarrrrr!

He reached the top, and licked a cloud.
"My stars are out. And I can touch one. See?"

"You did it!" said giant lion mom.

"Me too!" said Martin, and he leaped up and up from jungle ledge to jungle ledge, roaring,

Rrrrooooaaaaarrrr!

Gggrroooaaarrrr!

. . . up to the top,
where the jungle ledges met the stars,
where the moonlight hugged him,
where he could see the sky from edge to edge.

He touched a star up there
and scooped the night with his bucket.

19

Then Martin tugged at giant lion cub.
"Let's play. Take my bucket."

"We need rain in here," said the cub,
and he caught some cloud in the bucket.

Then they pounced back and forth
and up and down
on the highest jungle ledges
and roared the greatest jungle roars.

Ggrrooooaaarrr!

Rrrrooooaaa

Rrrrrooooaaa

22

23

And stopped roaring— shshshshsh—
to hear the sounds of the night,
the moon music, the star sighs,
until giant lion mom and giant lion dad
called to giant lion cub,
"Time to go! It will soon be light."

"Bye-bye," Martin said, as he watched them disappear.
Then he looked at everything under the stars,
the whole world from edge to edge,
the sleeping town, his own cozy house.

And right then, more than anything, he wanted to go home.

He slid from jungle ledge to jungle ledge
as morning light spread across the sandbox.
He hopped on his purple truck and sailed away,
all the way home, snuggling right in,
kissing Momma and Daddy good morning.

That afternoon in the sandbox
Martin searched for giant paw prints.
He didn't find any.
But in the sand
he found his bucket,
and still inside . . .

. . . was a puff of cloud with unfallen rain.